PERFECTLY NORMAN

TOM PERCIVAL

BLOOMSBURY

LONDON OXFORD NEW YORK NEW DELHI SYDNEY

DEDICATED to E.J.P.
(for being perfectly Ethan)

Bloomsbury Publishing, London, Oxford, New York, New Delhi and Sydney
First published in Great Britain in 2017 by Bloomsbury Publishing Plc
50 Bedford Square, London WC1B 3DP

www.bloomsbury.com

BLOOMSBURY is a registered trademark of Bloomsbury Publishing Plc

Text & illustrations copyright © Tom Percival 2017
The moral rights of the author/illustrator have been asserted

A CIP catalogue record of this book is available from the British Library

ISBN 978 1 4088 8096 8 (HB)
ISBN 978 1 4088 8097 5 (PB)
ISBN 978 1 4088 8098 2 (eBook)

All papers used by Bloomsbury Publishing are natural, recyclable products made from
wood grown in well managed forests. The manufacturing processes conform to the
environmental regulations of the country of origin.

Printed in China by Leo Paper Products, Heshan, Guangdong

10 9 8 7 6 5 4 3 2 1

Norman had always been normal
– *perfectly* normal.

Until one day . . .

...he grew a pair of wings!

Norman had imagined
growing taller . . .

or growing a beard,
like his dad . . .

But he had
never imagined
growing a pair of wings!

Still, they were here now, so he
decided to test them out right away.

Soon Norman was swooping around and generally having

the

MOST.

FUN.

EVER!

But then . . .

. . . he had to go in for dinner.

You see, Norman had always been SO normal
he didn't know how his parents would feel
about his *extraordinary* wings.

DINNER!

As he went in, Norman covered himself
up in a great big coat.

His parents didn't notice the wings . . .

But they *did* think it was odd to be
wearing a coat indoors!

Bath time was problematic.
So was bedtime.

The coat was hot and uncomfortable,
but Norman had decided that no one
should see his wings – *ever*.

The next day Norman went to the park,
but he was far too hot to play any
of his favourite games.

And so it went on . . .

Long car journeys were unbearable,

the swimming pool
was dreadful,

and that was *nothing* compared to his friend's birthday party.

The only time that Norman could feel normal now, was when it rained.

One day a boy tried to pull his coat off,

and Norman had to run away –
hot-faced, angry and sad.

He wished he'd *never* grown
those stupid wings.

Then he saw some birds, high up in the sky,
and remembered the joy of his first flight.

It occurred to Norman that it was
the *coat* that was making him
miserable, nOt the *wings*.

"Why don't you take that
tatty old thing off?" suggested
his mum and dad.

Norman looked up at
them hesitantly.

His parents smiled and nodded.
Norman smiled back.

Then he threw off the coat . . .

and let his wonderful
wings fan out.

Norman leapt into the air . . .

Finally he was free of that coat!

He noticed a few other children
wearing thick, heavy coats of their own.
They looked up at Norman and round
at each other nervously.

There was a moment's pause and then . . .

WHO

The sky was filled

OSH!

with flying people!

Norman had never
felt SO happy.

He realised that there was no such thing
as *perfectly normal* . . .

But he *was perfectly Norman.*
Which was just as it should be.